Guido van Genechten

Little White Fish Is So Happy

Clavis

NEW YORK

Little White Fish is so happy.
Mom is coming to get him!

Bye-bye, snail **in** the shell.

Bye-bye, frog **on** the rock.

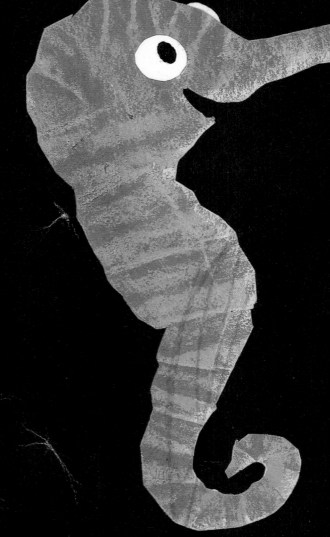

Bye-bye, seahorse under the leaf.

Bye-bye, crab **behind** the stone.

Bye-bye, goldfish
between the reeds.

Bye-bye friends, standing **next** to each other. I'm going home with mom.

But I'll be back tomorrow.

Mom, I am swimming in **front** of you!

First published in Belgium and Holland by Clavis Uitgeverij, Hasselt – Amsterdam, 2008
Copyright © 2008, Clavis Uitgeverij

English translation from the Dutch by Clavis Publishing Inc. New York
Copyright © 2017 for the English language edition: Clavis Publishing Inc. New York
Visit us on the web at www.clavisbooks.com

Little White Fish Is So Happy written and illustrated by Guido van Genechten
Original title: *Klein wit visje is zo blij*
Translated from the Dutch by Clavis Publishing

ISBN 978-1-60537-326-3

This book was printed in October 2016 at Publikum d.o.o., Slavka Rodica 6, Belgrade, Serbia

First Edition
10 9 8 7 6 5 4 3 2 1

Clavis Publishing supports the First Amendment and celebrates the right to read